This book belongs to

....

Copyright © 2016

make believe ideas ltd

The Wilderness, Berkhamsted, Hertfordshire, HP4 2AZ, UK.
501 Nelson Place, P.O. Box 141000, Nashville, TN 37214-1000, USA.

www.makebelieveideas.com

Written by Sarah Phillips.
Illustrated by Stuart Lynch.

Pennie the pinkest polar bear

Sarah Phillips · Stuart Lynch

make believe ideas

Pennie's a friendly polar bear,
but she is very, very shy.
She stammers as she says her name
and often starts to cry.

She blushes pink from head to toe
and can't think of what to say.
Who wants to play with a PINK bear?
So she usually runs away.

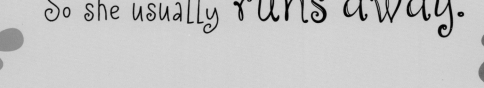

"You need to keep your **throat warm** with something **woolly** and **thick!**" says **Dan.** "My bark is **always** clear. This **scarf** will do the **trick.**"

"Now let's **stretch** and **twist** our necks
and try some **short**, sharp **sounds**."

So they **cough** and **bark** and stand up **tall**
and **wind** their **heads** around.

Later on a **cool** new **cat**
comes **sauntering** down the **street.**
Pennie runs up to say **hello,**
but **stammers** and **retreats.**

Cool Cat's shocked but understands. She knows just what to do.

"Come and drink my special milk. It'll soothe your throat for you."

Pennie and Cool Cat sip the milk,
warmed and mixed with honey.
They even try some "singing,"
but Dan doesn't find that funny!

As **Pennie** runs back through the **park,**
she meets the **Treetop Twins.**

"H-h-hi, I-I'M P-P-P-....!" she **stammers,**
before **escaping** to the **swings.**

The Treetop Twins
know how to help.
They say, "We have no doubt,
if you learn to say our
tongue-twisters,
it will sort the
stammering out!"

Just then the traveling pigs arrive
with big bags and a ball.
"H-hi, I'm P-P-P-...!" Pennie cries,
before her tears begin to fall.

"Come with us," the kind pigs say,
"Let's ALL have some fun.

We'll dance and sing together,
and join the others later on!"

"Pink is the perfect color!

That's what **we** both say.

Enjoy the fact that you turn pink

and hope to **stay** that **way!**"

As the **moon** shines in the sky
and **stars** start to **twinkle**,

the hushed friends inside the tent
hear **silver bells** that **tinkle** . . .

In comes Pennie, dressed in pink. She does a dance, and sings, "I'm Pennie the pinkest polar bear, and I want to say these things:

You're very welcome to the show. We hope you enjoy it all. There's dancing, music, acrobatics, and a very special ball!"

Pennie sits down, pink as pink,
and smiles at all her friends.
She's wowed by the amazing acts
and loves the mice at the end.

Pennie is walking home with Dan;
they're dancing as they go.

Don't be **upset** at how you are.
Enjoy yourself and **see**
that the **More** you gain in **confidence,**
the **happier** you'll be!